Nicola Davies
The Little Mistake

Illustrations Cathy Fisher

GRAFFEG

Rose raced up the sloping yard to the farmhouse at top speed. She kicked off her wellingtons, ran down the hall, and skidded into the kitchen door with a bang.

'People usually open doors first, Rose,' said Dad through a mouthful of chips.

'She's probably lost her teddy,' added Robert, and they both laughed. Sometimes Rose didn't like her dad and her big brother at all, and she was just about to tell them so when she felt a hand on her shoulder; it was Mum.

'What's the rush, Rosie Posie?' she said. 'I saw you tearing up the yard like a rabbit.'

Mum's face was a whole nest of wrinkles, but her dark eyes were as bright and alive as a robin's.

'Trixie's in the barn,' Rose told her, 'I think she's having her puppies!'

'Is she now!' Mum grinned. Trixie's pups were famous for miles around as the best sheepdogs in the county, and Mum was just as excited as Rose was about the new litter. 'Well, we'd better go an check on her!' said Mum.

'Can we have your chips then?' Dad and Robert called after them. Mum rolled her eyes.

'Those boys!' she said. 'What are they like?'

Mum collected the puppy bag from the hall cupboard. Inside was a lantern in case the birth lasted into the night and a medical kit to help Trixie or her pups if the birth was a difficult one.

'Don't know why I bother taking it though,' Mum laughed. 'Trixie never needs help.'

Mum and Rose slipped quietly in through the barn door and closed it behind them. The white flash on Trixie's nose showed in the dim light. She was lying on the floor, where she had swirled the hay into a kind of nest.

'How many pups d'you think she'll have this time?' Rose asked.

'She's old now, so maybe only three or four,' said Mum. 'But one of them could still be a champion!'

Some of Trixie's pups had won prizes at the county sheep dog trials. But as this would be her last litter, Mum had found an extra special mate for her, a fine collie dog called Bullet. Mum and Rose had high hopes for the puppies.

Trixie wagged her tail weakly and licked Mum's hand, but then lay still. Every few seconds she gave a little grunt as her tummy muscles tightened to help squeeze the puppies out.

'Won't be long now,' said Mum. 'She must have got to the barn just in time!'

Rose and Mum stroked Trixie's head and comforted her during her contractions, expecting any minute to see the first little wet bundle of puppy appear from Trixie's bottom.

But no puppies came. Blackbirds sang their last songs in the spring dusk and it grew dark; and Rose lit the gas lantern, but still no puppies came.

Trixie began to look very tired.

'Poor old girl,' said Mum, 'lets see what's happening, shall we?'

Mum had helped with hundreds of litters of puppies. The vet always said she knew more about dogs giving birth than he did. She put a surgical glove on her right hand and very gently felt inside Trixie. Rose held a torch to give her extra light.

'Oh dear,' said Mum, 'no wonder you've had so much trouble, Trix. These pups are huge.'

Mum pulled out one pup and then another. Rose didn't want to look at them. She was glad Mum put the bodies straight behind the bale where Trixie wouldn't see them. Rose bit her lip. She knew she had to be brave. Crying now wouldn't help.

'There's just one more to come,' said Mum. 'But it's even bigger. I'm going to have to pull hard. Keep the torch steady now, Rose.'

Mum got hold of the pup and the next time Trixie had a contraction, she pulled. Trixie seemed to know that Mum was trying to help and put every bit of strength she had left into pushing.

'Come on, Trix!' Mum said.

Then there was a slurping sound, and it was over. Trixie went limp, Mum fell back on the hay, and Rose sat down in a heap.

The only one of them who seemed full of life was the puppy. It lay in a wet dollop on the hay, still half-covered in the see-through sac of skin that had held it safe in Trixie's tummy. It squirmed and let out a loud squeak. At once, Trixie turned to the pup and began to lick it. Her strong pink tongue pummelled and pounded its body, like hands kneading dough. The puppy squeaked more loudly, but its little voice kept being smothered by Trixie's licking. It sounded like someone trying to whistle under water.

'There's no doubt it's alive,' said Mum. 'Though what sort of dog it is I don't know.'

Now that the puppy was clean, Rose could see that it didn't look anything like a sheepdog. Instead of being black and white with sleek, smooth fur, its coat was pale and rough, like dirty wool.

'I don't know whose puppy you are,' Mum told it, ' but you certainly aren't Bullet's. Trixie must slipped off and mated with another dog on the sly. Oh, Trix!'

Mum sounded so disappointed, Rose was glad that it was dim enough in the barn to hide the hot blush that spread over her face; this pup was her fault. The day before Bullet

had been brought to mate with Trixie, Rose had taken her for a walk. 'Don't let her off the lead,' Mum had said, but Trix whined so much that Rose had given in and let her run free. The moment she was free, Trixie disappeared. Rose had called and called, but Trix didn't come back for two hours. That must have been when it had happened!

It was almost midnight. Trixie had taken six hours to give birth to one funny-looking puppy that would never win anything at all! Mum looked sadly at the fuzzy white body, cuddled up to Trixie's belly.

'Bit of a mistake, aren't you, pup?' she told it, and shook her head.

Rose woke early. Outside, she could hear Dad and Robert driving the tractors and trailers off down the lane. They worked together for all the other farms around and about, cutting grass to make into silage, winter feed for cattle and sheep. They would be gone until well after dark.

Sunshine poured in through her window and birds sang. It was going to be a lovely day. But instead of bouncing out of bed as usual, Rose crept from under the duvet, slow as a slug, with a cold puddle of guilt and disappointment sloshing inside her.

Mum was in the kitchen when Rose went down. She liked 'a bit of peace' first thing, so Rose made herself a plate of toast and sat listening to the ticking of the old clock on the dresser. At last, Mum spoke.

'Shame about that pup,' she said.

Rose knew now was the time to tell Mum that Trixie's odd pup was all her fault. But instead she cut her toast into four perfect triangles and looked at her plate.

After breakfast, Mum sent Rose to feed Trixie. Inside the barn, streaks of sunlight made the dust dance in the air over the dog's head.

'Here you are, girl,' said Rose. Trixie opened her eyes and sniffed at the bowl. She struggled to her feet, gulped the food down in ten seconds then lapped a whole bowl of water. The pup was fast asleep in the nest of hay. Trixie seemed to understand that Rose could be babysitter, so she slipped outside to wee on the grass at the back of the barn.

While she was gone, Rose looked at the pup. Curled up with its blunt baby nose tucked into the stubby puppy tail, it looked sweet. Its coat was a mass of little fluffy curls the colour of whipped cream, its legs were long and its paws looked as if they were several sizes too large; Rose knew that puppies grew into their paws, so it was clear this pup was going to be a very big dog indeed. She couldn't imagine who the dad had been.

The pup was dreaming. Its paws were moving and its body was twitching. Whatever could a newborn pup dream about? Rose wondered. Perhaps it was dreaming about the life it was going to have. Rose reached out and touched the pup very gently on its head.

'A bit of a mistake.'

Once, long ago, Mum had said almost the same thing about her! Rose had been too small to talk then, but she remembered hearing Mum telling Aunty Sylvia.

'Rose was our little mistake,' she'd said. *Our little mistake;* what did it mean? Rose wondered. It didn't seem very nice to begin your life as a mistake.

Trixie came back and lay down next to her sleeping baby.

'I like your pup, Trix,' Rose whispered. Trixie licked the back of Rose's hand, then laid her head on her paws and went to sleep.

Just as they were about to leave for school, Mum's mobile rang. It was Dad; the big tractor had broken down and he needed her to bring him some tools and spare parts.

'I'll drop you at school, and go straight there,' Mum said. 'Don't know what I'll do about the shearer though. He's due here at ten-thirty and I won't have time to get the sheep penned for him.'

Mum's face creased in worry. It was hard to get the shearer to come to a small flock like theirs; somehow they *had* to be ready. Before she'd even thought it, Rose said, 'I'll get the sheep penned, Mum.'

'Are you sure, Rosie Posie?'

Rose wasn't really sure, but it seemed too late to say that now.

'I know what to do.'

Mum frowned, then smiled.

'Alright. Give it a try.'

'I can be a bit late for school, can't I?'

'Of course,' said Mum. 'I'll write you a note.'

Rose let Bobby, Mum's second sheepdog, out of her pen in the first of the old stable boxes. Bobby was one of Trixie's daughters, bigger and stronger than her Mum, but not as bold or swift. She bounded around Rose's legs, delighted to be out in the sunshine. Rose was nervous. Mum had taught her how to work with sheep and dogs as soon as she was big enough to walk and blow into a whistle, but she'd never done it without Mum standing by. Rose bit her lip; she had to do this job well, to make up a little bit for Trixie's pup. She took a deep breath.

'C'mon, Bobby!' she said.

As Rose and Bobby neared the gate into the meadow, Bobby grew quiet and sharp. Like all good sheepdogs, she knew that once in the field she was on duty.

Lord's Meadow was on the steepest bit of hillside, with bracken and brambles in clumps around its edges. The flock

were at the very top, grazing busily. Rose's job was to get the sheep into the pen in the shady corner by the gate.

Mum's flock was small, just twenty ewes and their lambs, but once there had been more than two thousand sheep on Ridge Farm.

'They filled the whole yard on shearing day,' Mum had told her. There was an old photo on the dresser of a young Mum and Dad and a very small Robert standing in a sea of woolly backs, with big grins on all their faces. But something had gone wrong. When Rose was just a month old, the big flock was sold and Dad took to working with machines instead of sheep. No one talked about it, but Rose wondered if her birth had somehow brought bad luck to Ridge Farm. Was that what Mum had meant by *'Rose is our little mistake'*?

Rose and Bobby stepped into the field. Rose looked down at Bobby. The dog was staring up at the sheep, trembling with energy, absolutely dying to get going! Rose felt better; at least Bobby knew what to do!

The little flat whistle tasted of Mum's face cream. It was cold on Rose's lips. She took a big breath and blew. The sound was almost too high to hear, but Bobby knew just what it meant; she set off like a rocket, a blur of black and white streaking over the bright grass.

Rose blew again, to steady the dog. If she ran straight at

the sheep they'd panic and scatter, and then it would take all morning to get them penned. The trick was to keep them calm, moving together in a tight flock. But Bobby was too excited, and Rose had made her command too late. Bobby raced up to the sheep and they ran in all directions.

'Lie down! Lie down!' Rose yelled. Bobby dropped to the ground and lay with her ears flat to her head. The sheep stood, nervous and staring, ready to bolt again. Rose held her breath. Slowly, they calmed, put their heads down and began to graze.

Mum always said that working a dog with sheep was like tuning into a radio station, you had to find the place where the signal was crystal clear.

'It's all about paying attention, Rose,' Mum had said. 'You have to concentrate.' Rose put the whistle to her lips again and concentrated hard, watching Bobby very carefully so that her commands came at just the right moment. Now, when she whistled, the dog reacted at once, trotting backwards and forwards across the slope of the field, gently pushing the flock towards the pen. Rose felt a tingle, as if an invisible thread ran through the shining air between her and the sheepdog.

The last stretch before the pen was tricky. One of the ewes was startled and stood tense, all set to run in panic. Rose made Bobby freeze until the sheep got its confidence back. Then, just as if they were guided by the palm of a big hand, the flock trotted sweetly into their pen and Rose clattered the gate shut behind them. The sound seemed to echo right over the top of the hills, up into the mounds of puffy clouds blowing in the sky above.

Mum was very pleased with Rose. She kept smiling at her and saying well done. They drove to school singing 'Ten Green Bottles', with the car windows down and the spring air rushing in over their faces.

'And if one green bottle should accidentally fall...' sang Rose.

'There'd be no green bottles hanging on the wall!' Mum sang back, smiling. The cold pool of bad feeling inside Rose shrank to a tiny puddle; getting the sheep penned had made up, at least a little bit, for the puppy.

The car stopped outside school and Mum turned to look at her.

'I've been thinking,' she said. 'It's about time you had a dog of your own to train.' Rose's heart leapt.

'I was going to give you the best of Trix's pups,' Mum's voice trailed off, her smile gone and last night's disappointment all over her face. Rose looked down at her school bag while the icy pool inside grew back to a lake. How was she going to tell Mum about letting Trix off the lead that day?

'Anyway,' Mum began again. 'I could buy you one of Bullet's pups instead!'

Bullet's pups would be perfect sheep dogs. Rose imagined a black and white silky head under her hand, and a dog called Shadow or Lighting running up the hillside at her command. But that thought only made the cold feeling worse, so Rose said something that even she found rather surprising.

'Don't buy me a dog. I'll train Trixie's pup.'

The first problem was what to call him. Border collie names just didn't seem right for a dollop of white fluff! But white fluffy names were no good for a working dog. For the next three months, whilst the pup grew and grew, Rose tried out every name she could think of.

'What about Snowball?' she said one evening over supper.

Dad groaned.

'We're not talking about names again, are we?'

'What about Killer?' said Robert.

Rose just stared at her brother; he was hopeless.

'Might help if you knew who the father was,' said Dad.

'Well, that's just a mystery,' said Mum, 'there isn't a dog round here who looks even a bit like him. I can't think where Trixie found a mate like that.' Mum laughed, a real laugh Rose was glad to see, and Dad and Robert were smiling too.

You couldn't really help smiling when you thought about Trixie's pup. To start with there was the way he looked, like a giant, lollopy ball of wool, already more than half the size of his Mum and covered in perfect little cream kiss curls of fur. He had all the energy of a sheepdog puppy but none of their excitability; he was always calm, 'laid back', Dad said.

Everyone who met Trixie's pup loved him and he loved them right back. In the morning the pup kept Mum company in the veg garden, or trotted along and sat beside Robert mending a tractor, or Dad doing the accounts in the farm office; he was always there to see Rose off to school and waiting at the gate, wagging his tail when she came home. Nobody ever mentioned the fact that he was a mistake, not even Mum.

By the time the summer holidays came round and Rose had time to try training her rather odd sheepdog, no one had to think of a name for him anymore; he already had one that they all used: Puppy.

Puppy learned fast. He had two lessons a day, away from his Mum. He learned 'sit' and 'stay' and 'lie down' and 'come', all in just a week. Rose got Mum out in the yard to show her what he could do.

'Puppy, lie down,' said Rose. Puppy dropped onto his tummy.

'Puppy, stay,' Rose said sternly and walked away, leaving him at the bottom of the yard whilst she walked back up to Mum, standing by the back door.

'That's very good for such a young pup,' said Mum. 'Trix wouldn't have stayed so solid at that age.' Puppy was still in the same spot, lying down as if he'd been glued. Rose was very proud.

'Puppy, come!' Rose called, and he leapt up at once and rushed across the yard like lightning.

'Good dog, Puppy. Well done!' She buried her face in his fluffiness. Mum fussed him too.

'Well,' said Mum, 'I think we should show him the sheep tomorrow, and see what he does.'

It was a chilly, overcast day, with scrappy clouds like ripped grey socks rushing low over the hills. But it showed off the deep greens of late summer so beautifully that Rose didn't mind having to wear a sweater. Working sheep was better in the cool anyway.

Rose and Mum walked around the hill to the sheep with all three dogs – Bobby and Trixie free and Puppy on a lead, with his first collar.

'There's still a good bit of grass in this field,' said Mum. 'But it won't hurt to move the sheep into the next one. I'll work the dogs, you take Puppy up there where he can see and hear what happens.'

'C'mon then, Pup.' Rose pulled on the lead and Puppy
came, looking over his shoulder at his mum, obviously not
sure what was happening. Rose took him quietly to the
top of the field. Below them the ewes and their half-
grown lambs, almost fifty sheep altogether, grazed in
a loose gang. Puppy had never really seen sheep
before, certainly not this close, and he was
very interested indeed. He stared at them,
his body tense, his floppy round ears
pricked and his tail out like an
antenna. The breeze

began to blow in their faces. Rose could smell the sheep and she knew that the scent would be ten times stronger for Puppy with his sensitive doggy nose. He lifted his snout into the air, taking long thoughtful sniffs and narrowing his big dark eyes. His expression reminded her of Mum reading the paper: he was fascinated! Rose's heart beat fast. Surely this was a sign that Puppy would be a great sheepdog!

Mum sent the dogs off, each with their own whistled command. It had been a while since Rose had seen her Mum working two dogs, and Trixie was a little out of practice. All the same, it was magical to watch. Mum could read the hillside like the pages of a book – the rolling dips and ridges of the field, the mood of the flock, the bodies of the running dogs.

She directed her commands so well that Bobby and Trixie must have felt as if her voice was inside their heads. The dogs swirled gently around the flock, conducting them down the hillside towards the gate like a dance.

Rose was so absorbed in watching that she didn't feel Puppy's lead slip from her hand. So, when a darting white shape appeared on the hillside running straight for the centre of the flock, she didn't realise for a moment what it was.

There was no point trying to call him, the wind was blowing hard and would carry her voice away. In any case, she could see by the way he ran, with his tail out and his nose held forward, that nothing was going to stop him. Puppy was going to run right into the centre of the flock. They'd scatter and he'd chase them. It was a disaster! Mum would be furious.

But when Puppy reached the bunched flock, the sheep didn't take any notice of him at all. They stayed together and moved as Bobby and Trixie drove them, with Puppy in the middle of them just like another sheep.

'Well, he isn't going to be much of a dog if they don't even notice he's there!' Dad laughed when he heard the story of Puppy's first meeting with the flock.

'Maybe he'll learn to talk to them!'

Robert and Dad collapsed into giggles again. Rose could see that Mum wanted to join in, though she was trying not to.

'Don't take it to heart, Rose, love,' she said. 'He's still a lovely dog, even if he can't herd sheep. I'll get you one of Bullet's pups like I promised.'

'I don't want one of Bullet's pups!' Rose shouted. 'I want Puppy.'

Rose got up from the table and stomped upstairs. Outside in the yard Puppy was greeting Big Merv from the farm next door, waving his fluffy tail at him like a flag. Stupid dog, thought Rose. Didn't he know everyone was laughing at him? She shut her curtains and turned her radio on loud.

Rose didn't know how long she'd been asleep, but it was dark when she woke. The TV was on downstairs; Mum and Dad were probably dozing off in front of some boring gardening programme, and Robert was out.

She went down into the yard, where moonlight shone bright as day. The dogs had been shut into the loose boxes for the night and everything was quiet.

But Puppy snuffled behind his door. Rose had been so angry with him that she hadn't seen him all day. He whined a little and Rose felt sorry. It wasn't his fault that he wasn't a sheepdog, like Bullet's pups would have been. She called his name softly and let him out. He wagged his tail and licked her hand. Rose took his lead off the hook by the door.

'C'mon, Puppy, lets go for a walk.'

She took him down the lane, away from the fields where the Ridge Farm flock were, over the bridge and up the hill to the common where she could let him run.

Puppy was so happy to be out. He sniffed and snuffled at every plant and bush and trotted beside her without once straining the lead. Mum was right, he was a lovely dog. Maybe it didn't matter that he was just a pet and not a working dog. Yet somehow Rose couldn't get that word *mistake* out of her head.

It was beautiful on the common. A wide velvet sky and silvery hills off into the distance forever and ever. She sat in the grass and looked and looked. Puppy looked with her, his warm fluffy body leaning against hers, his nose lifted to read the air.

He was a good dog, and he deserved a little freedom before being shut up for the night. Rose got up and unclipped his lead. She walked a little way and Puppy trotted nearby, and then, suddenly, out went his tail, up went his nose, and before Rose could say 'Puppy' once, he was gone.

She searched up and down the common. She called, but not very loud. She didn't want anyone to know he was loose up here.

At last, she shoved the lead in her pocket and ran home, hoping no one had noticed she'd been gone.

It was only just light when Rose heard the banging on the door. Mum and Dad must have heard it sooner, because they were both halfway down the stairs before Rose. The three of them opened the back door together. There was Big Merv, hunched in the early drizzle with Puppy on a lead of string. Puppy was soaking wet and there was a blob of blood on his nose.

Rose felt sick. If Puppy had been caught chasing sheep he'd have to be shot. That was the rule. But Merv was smiling, a big gap-toothed smile.

'Well,' he said cheerily. 'Great to have a welcoming committee. Guess what? Turns out your little mistake is a bit of a hero!'

Mum, Dad and Rose looked at each other then back at Merv.

'You going to ask me in for a cup of tea or stand there with your mouths open like fish out of water?'

Merv had five cups of tea with two sugars and a huge plate of toast and honey. He deserved it; he'd been out all night watching his sheep.

'I lost eight lambs in the last week. I knew it was dogs. Strays, I suppose. So I've been keeping an eye out at night, watching the flock.'

Merv took a big bite of toast and another swig of tea.

'Anyway, last night, the sheep were very quiet. Almost dozed off myself. Then, just about first light, these two big mongrels come up, going for my sheep. And who pops up from the middle of the flock? Pup here! He must've been there all along and I just didn't notice him, and neither did the sheep.'

Merv laughed.

'Pup got his teeth into one of the strays, then chased them over two fields. I never seen two dogs more scared!'

Mum shook her head and smiled.

'Reckon you could do worse than breed a few more of him, Ruby!' said Merv. Dad slipped Puppy a slice of buttered toast when Mum wasn't looking; he winked, and Rose winked back.

It was still summer in September, so it felt weird going back to school. Especially a new school, with a bus to catch to get to it. Everyone came to the farm gate to see her off, Mum, Dad, Robert and Puppy waving his big tail like a flag.

Rose walked down the lane to the bus stop. A girl in new school uniform like Rose's was already there, with her mum. Next to them on the end of a smart leather lead was a dog, huge and white with kiss curl fur. The girl said her name was Natalie; she seemed nice but a bit shy. The mum wasn't shy at all.

'It's so nice to meet you, Rose,' she said. 'We've just moved in but we've met lots of people already. Everyone round here seems so friendly! Berja here made friends with a lovely sheepdog on the very first day we saw our new home, didn't you, boy?'

Suddenly Rose found she couldn't say a word.

'I think sheepdogs always like other sheepdogs,' Natalie's mum went on. 'In Italy they use dogs like him to protect sheep from wolves, you know. Oh, now here's the bus...'

Rose and Natalie sat together on the bus.

'Sorry about my mum,' said Natalie, 'she's mad about our dog!'

Rose was staring through the gap in the curtains at the stars when Mum called in on her way to bed.

'Still awake Rose?' said Mum.

'I've got something to tell you, Mum,' said Rose in a small voice. 'It's about Puppy.'

Mum listened to the story of how Trixie had run off, and all about the big white dog at the bus stop, but she didn't seem cross at all.

'It sounds to me,' Mum said, 'as if Trixie knew exactly what she was doing. I think she knew all along that Puppy would be special.'

Rose nodded.

'He is special, isn't he, Mum?'

'Very special,' said Mum. 'Just like you, Rose.'

'But I thought I was a mistake.'

Mum sighed and took Rose's hand in hers.

'It's true that we hadn't planned to have another baby,' Mum said. 'We thought we were just too old. And it was a bad time for the farm. We were selling the sheep and going to work on other people's farms. Dad and I were worn out and worried. And then you came, Rose. You came, and you were so sweet that you just made everything all right.'

Mum smiled her best bird-bright smile and hugged Rose tight, 'Sometimes the things you don't plan are the best of all!' she said.

'Like Puppy,' said Rose.

'Yes,' said Mum. 'Like Puppy, and you.'

Nicola Davies

Nicola is an award-winning author whose many books for children include *The Promise* (Green Earth Book Award 2015, CILIP Kate Greenaway Medal Shortlist 2015), *Tiny* (AAAS/Subaru SB&F Prize 2015), *A First Book of Nature*, *Whale Boy* (Blue Peter Book Awards Shortlist 2014), and the Heroes of the Wild series (Portsmouth Book Award 2014).

She graduated in Zoology, studied whales and bats and then worked for the BBC Natural History Unit. Underlying all Nicola's writing is the belief that a relationship with nature is essential to every human being, and that now, more than ever, we need to renew that relationship.

Nicola's children's books from Graffeg include *Perfect* (2017 CILIP Kate Greenaway Medal Longlist), *The Pond* (2018 CILIP Kate Greenaway Medal Longlist), the Shadows and Light series, *The Word Bird, Animal Surprises* and *Into the Blue.*

Cathy Fisher

Cathy Fisher grew up with eight brothers and sisters, playing in the fields overlooking Bath.

She has been a teacher and practising artist all her life, living and working in the UK, Seychelles and Australia.

Art is Cathy's first language. As a young child she scribbled on the walls of her bedroom and ever since has felt a sense of urgency to paint and draw stories which she feels need to be heard and expressed.

Cathy's first published books with Graffeg include *Perfect*, followed by *The Pond*, written by Nicola Davies. Both books were Longlisted for the CILIP Kate Greenaway Medal.

Graffeg Childrens' Books

Perfect
Nicola Davies
Illustrations by Cathy Fisher

The Pond
Nicola Davies
Illustrations by Cathy Fisher

The White Hare
Nicola Davies
Illustrated by Anastasia Izlesou

Mother Cary's Butter Knife
Nicola Davies
Illustrations by Anja Uhren

Elias Martin
Nicola Davies
Illustrations by Fran Shum

The Selkie's Mate
Nicola Davies
Illustrations by Claire Jenkins

Bee Boy and the Moonflowers
Nicola Davies
Illustrations by Max Low

The Eel Question
Nicola Davies
Illustrations by Beth Holland

Graffeg Childrens' Books

Gaspard The Fox
Zeb Soanes, Illustrations by James Mayhew

Ootch Cootch
Malachy Doyle, Illustrations by Hannah Doyle

Through the Eyes of Me
Jon Roberts, Illustrations by Hannah Rounding

The Knight Who Took all Day
James Mayhew

The Animal Surprises series
by Nicola Davies, Illustrations by Abbie Cameron
The Word Bird, Animal Surprises, Into the Blue

Celestine and the Hare series
by Karin Celestine
Small Finds a Home, Paper Boat for Panda, Honey for Tea,
Catching Dreams, A Small Song, Finding Your Place,
Bertram Likes to Sew, Bert's Garden

How to Draw series
by Nicola Davies, Illustrations by Abbie Cameron
The Word Bird How to Draw, Animal Surprises How to Draw,
Into the Blue How to Draw

Paradise Found
John Milton, Illustrations by Helen Elliott

The Little Mistake
Published in Great Britain in 2018
by Graffeg Limited

Written by Nicola Davies
copyright © 2018.
Illustrated by Cathy Fisher
copyright © 2018.
Designed and produced by Graffeg
Limited copyright © 2018.

Graffeg Limited, 24 Stradey Park
Business Centre, Mwrwg Road,
Llangennech, Llanelli, Carmarthenshire
SA14 8YP Wales UK
Tel 01554 824000 www.graffeg.com

A CIP Catalogue record for this book is
available from the British Library.

ISBN 9781912654086

1 2 3 4 5 6 7 8 9